The Big Bad Wolf

D0711977

retold by Pam Holden
illustrated by Kelvin Hawley

WITHDRAWN

1

One day a little girl was walking
through the forest.
Her name was Little Red Riding Hood.
She was going to visit her Grandma,
with a basket of food for her.

2

The Big Bad Wolf was hiding
behind a tree in the forest.
He saw Little Red Riding Hood
with her basket.
"Grrr!" he growled. "I'm hungry.
I want to eat all the food
in that basket!"

4

He ran fast to Grandma's house,
and he knocked on the door.
Knock! Knock! Knock!
Grandma was very frightened
when she saw the wolf.

Property Of
Wisconsin School for the Deaf

Grandma ran into her bedroom.
"The wolf is coming!" she cried.
"Where can I hide?"
She hid from him just in time.

8

The wolf put on some of
Grandma's clothes.
Then he got into her bed.
Soon Little Red Riding Hood
knocked on the door.
"Come in," called the wolf
from Grandma's bedroom.

Little Red Riding Hood cried,
"Oh, Grandma, what big ears
you have!"
The wolf said, "All the better
to hear you with."
"But Grandma, what big eyes
you have!" cried Little Red
Riding Hood.
"All the better to see what's
in your basket," said the wolf.

Little Red Riding Hood cried,
"But Grandma, what big teeth
you have!"
The wolf growled, "All the better
to eat the food in your basket!"
Little Red Riding Hood ran to
the window to get help.
She saw her father in the forest.
"Help, Dad! Help me!" she called.

15

Her father ran inside the house
to help Little Red Riding Hood.
Grandma said, "Thank you!
You got here just in time.
Now let's see what's in that basket."